W9-BRZ-286

/
R983c

CHILDREN OF CHRISTMAS

A RICHARD JACKSON BOOK

By Cynthia Rylant

PICTURE BOOKS

Birthday Presents
Night in the Country
The Relatives Came
This Year's Garden
Miss Maggie
When I Was Young in the Mountains

"The Henry and Mudge Books"
———
Henry and Mudge
Henry and Mudge in Puddle Trouble
Henry and Mudge in the Green Time

STORIES

Children of Christmas
Every Living Thing

POETRY

Waiting to Waltz: A Childhood

NOVELS

A Fine White Dust
A Blue-Eyed Daisy

Children of Christmas

STORIES FOR THE SEASON

by Cynthia Rylant

DRAWINGS BY S. D. SCHINDLER

ORCHARD BOOKS
A division of Franklin Watts, Inc.
New York / London

Text copyright © 1987 by Cynthia Rylant
Illustrations copyright © 1987 by S. D. Schindler
All rights reserved. No part of this book may be reproduced or transmitted
in any form or by any means, electronic or mechanical, including
photocopying, recording or by any information storage or retrieval
system, without permission in writing from the Publisher.

Orchard Books
387 Park Avenue South
New York, NY 10016

Orchard Books Canada
20 Torbay Road
Markham, Ontario 23P1G6

Orchard Books is a division of Franklin Watts, Inc.

Manufactured in the United States of America
Book design by Mina Greenstein
The text of this book is set in 12 pt. Goudy Old Style.
The illustrations are pencil drawings, reproduced in halftone.
1   3   5   7   9   10   8   6   4   2

Library of Congress Cataloging-in-Publication Data
Rylant, Cynthia. Children of Christmas.
Contents: The Christmas tree man—Halfway home—For being good—
[etc.]   1. Christmas stories.   2. Children's stories, American.
[1. Christmas—Fiction.   2. Short stories]   I. Schindler, S. D.,
ill.   II. Title.
PZ7.R982Ch   1987   [Fic]   87-1690
ISBN 0-531-05706-2   ISBN 0-531-08306-3 (lib. bdg.)

+
R983c

7 20

Gordon

10-19-87

For my dear family of choice

Contents

———

The
Christmas Tree
Man

HIS HOUSE is far out. Farther out than you can imagine anyone living. It's small and clean and white. Most summers it's cool; most winters it's warm.

It's a good house for a man alone.

The man himself is a small man, and skinny. He has never married. He has no one. And each year, he grows older.

He didn't know he would live his life alone. When he was a boy, and his name was Garnet Ash, he lived with his family on a street in a town not too big. He was a regular boy. He played football and he fished and he camped out in his backyard. But because he loved being at home most of all, he had few friends and spent most of his days with his parents. Each night he fell asleep listening to their soft voices moving from room to room.

But before Garnet Ash had barely grown up, quite suddenly, his parents died. And Garnet Ash didn't know what to do with himself, with them gone, his family. He hadn't had time to find a wife. And with suddenly no family to whom he could bring a wife, with suddenly no father who could build a nice kitchen table for her, with suddenly no mother who could give summer roses to her . . . with suddenly no one at all, Garnet Ash didn't know what to do except go on having no one at all.

He couldn't live in his town any longer. He missed his father and mother too much. So he found a small white house far out, and he moved away, farther out than you can imagine.

And he found an occupation that kept him living, that has kept him living so many, many years.

Garnet Ash is a Christmas Tree Man. Now, few people know him by his real name. They know him only as the Christmas Tree Man.

All around his small white house grow those Christmas trees. Garnet Ash plants them and he raises them like children. Some fat, some lopsided, some strong like rocks and others too weak to try anymore.

Like anything else, his trees bring him joy and sorrow.

At certain times of the year, Garnet Ash will drive his old truck out and into the towns to get groceries and fertilizer and kerosene and saplings. But apart from these few trips into the world of grocers and farmers and nurserymen, Garnet Ash lives out each of his years alone.

In March, when purple crocuses spurt up through the snow, he stands and admires them alone. In June, when hornets build a nest under the eaves of his house, he stands and worries alone. And in October, when the moon is giant and orange, he stands and whispers to it alone. He often thinks of his parents.

And all this time, his children are growing.

But Garnet Ash, who spends his birthdays alone, who eats Thanks-

giving dinner alone, who watches the beginnings of each winter and spring and summer and fall alone—come December, he will be surrounded.

They drive out from the towns in their cars to find him. The cars are shiny and white or red or yellow. In them there is always more than one person and usually there are three or four or five.

They are families. They need a Christmas tree. And they have come looking for the Christmas Tree Man.

Garnet Ash expects them. Every year. And even after all these many years of seeing them drive up to his small, clean white house, he has not grown tired of them.

On the first day of December Garnet Ash is full of anticipation. He trembles with it. He stands before his mirror and trims his hair, combs his beard, plucks his brows a bit. He reaches into the back of a drawer and pulls forth his best red reindeer scarf.

He is looking forward to the company.

The people park their shiny cars and the doors open and out they climb, mothers and fathers and children and grandparents, and they are filled up with life, with hope, with wanting a tree.

The Christmas Tree Man in the red reindeer scarf welcomes them and they say hello, how are you, getting cold isn't it, do you have a good crop this year?

And Garnet Ash gestures to his fields, he introduces his children, he says, "I have a good crop."

So the men and the women and the children and even sometimes the dogs they have brought with them will hurry into the rows and rows of sleeping green trees, quiet green trees. The snow will crack under their boots and the mist of their breathing will rise up to the sky and they will prowl through the fields of the Christmas Tree Man.

Garnet Ash is happy. He is proud. He says "Merry Christmas!" and waves to them as they drive off, their shiny cars sprouting bushy pine tails. Sometimes a boy will lean out of a car window, waving, and the eyes of Garnet Ash will soften and his smile will slacken and he will think he is waving to himself. To himself and his family driving off in that car.

The cars will keep coming, every day, and at night, too. Everyone looking for the Christmas Tree Man. And when all of his best trees are gone and there is nothing to offer but a lopsided tree, a skinny tree, a short tree, Garnet Ash will give the people bags of hot chestnuts to ease their disappointment. Eating chestnuts, they'll decide a lopsided tree isn't so bad, really.

Finally, on Christmas Eve, there will be only one or two cars.

Then, Garnet Ash will be alone.

Very late in the night on Christmas Eve, he will walk through his fields, among the stumps and the trees left behind.

"So, not pretty enough for them, eh?" he will say to one of his children. "Well, lucky for you, I'd say!"

He will walk through the stumps and the trees, and the moon will be large and white and the sky clear and deep, and the rabbits will watch him from the edges of his fields.

Garnet Ash will walk until he finds the weakest tree among those left to stand, the sorriest tree. And he will unwind his red reindeer scarf from around his neck and he will drape it on the top boughs of his ugly child.

Then, very late, Garnet Ash will walk back to his small, clean white house and he will smile to himself and think what it is to be a Christmas Tree Man.

Halfway Home

HER FATHER is ordering eggs and toast as he warms his hands over his coffee cup. Frances wants only a piece of cherry pie. And hot chocolate. The diner is steamy with the aroma of fried potatoes and hamburger grease, and its foggy windows hide the snow outside.

It is, for Frances, like a long, skinny, smelly cocoon this Christmas Eve. She is wrapped with her father into this safe, warm place.

They have just picked up the sewing machine for her mother, and Frances thinks of it in its box in the trunk of the car. The machine is black, with gold designs. It is very elegant. Her mother will love them for buying it.

It is already dark outside. Frances is usually home at this time on Christmas Eve. But the drive to the city was long, and so many cars, and waiting in line at the sewing machine store. She and her father are only halfway home now. Maybe they should have kept driving. But they were so hungry . . .

Frances watches the waitress fry her father's eggs. The woman has a round sun face and dove eyes and her long blonde hair is pulled back tight, running to her waist. Frances watches her and wonders if she will fry eggs here all night, and if someone will have a surprise present for her on Christmas morning.

Only four people are eating in the diner this Christmas Eve. Frances, her father, a big man in a plaid coat, and a thin young man with a beard. The young man has a paperback book in his left hand, and he reads it while he spoons chili into his mouth with his right. The big man just stares at nothing while he drinks his coffee.

When the waitress sets the food they ordered in front of Frances and her father, she smiles at Frances and squirts a giant dollop of whipped cream atop the hot chocolate. It's the most whipped cream Frances has ever had on hot chocolate and her eyes are very big.

Christmas music plays on the diner's radio, hot coffee brews, and the five people in the cocoon are quiet with their thoughts and their hunger this night.

Suddenly, Frances sees a shadow at one of the diner's windows. She looks hard. The shadow has a tail.

"Daddy, look. A cat!"

Frances' father and the waitress and the big man and the young man all turn to the window where Frances is pointing. The shadow's tail moves back and forth on the foggy glass.

Everyone in the diner looks at everyone else for a moment. They look back at the window. They look at each other again. Finally, the waitress comes from behind the counter and opens the door.

"Here, kitty," she calls.

And quicker than anyone expects, the shadow with a tail is gone and a black cat is walking in the door.

The cat is long and skinny, like the diner, and the top of its head is sprinkled with snowflakes. Its large green eyes look directly into the eyes of the waitress, then, rubbing against her legs, the cat squeaks out a meow.

"Goodness sakes," says the waitress.

The big man in the plaid coat says it first:

"Looks hungry."

Frances looks at her father's plate full of eggs, then she looks at her father. He gives her a What-do-you-mean-give-that-cat-my-eggs? look.

The sun-faced waitress scoops the cat up in her arms. She says to everybody in the diner, "This cat's not supposed to be here, you know."

Everybody nods his head.

"Against health regulations," she says, scratching the cat behind its ear.

Everybody nods again. No one speaks. Then the young man says, "You think it'll eat chili?"

He holds his bowl out to the waitress.

Everybody laughs then and they all say something about it being Christmas and what kind of regulations would keep a hungry cat outside, and the waitress is setting the cat back on the floor again, offering it the warm safety of her diner.

Frances jumps off her stool and goes to the cat. They all watch as the cat rubs against her, pushing its nose into her hair. Frances' father lets his eggs get cold as he watches her with bright eyes.

When the waitress puts a saucer of milk on the counter, Frances lifts the cat up. Everyone watches the animal drink deep and long, and the big man says "About starved" and the young man says "Pretty animal" and the waitress says "Poor thing."

After drinking the milk, the cat walks up and down the length of the counter, stepping over salt and pepper shakers, circling coffee cups, to say hello to everyone. The waitress, who is frying a hamburger for the animal, looks alarmed at first, but the diner's customers are all smiling and laughing and reaching out to touch the soft black fur. She lets the cat walk.

Finally the big man says, "Well, who's going to take it home?"

Everyone except Frances shrugs his shoulders and watches the cat eat the little pieces of hamburger the waitress has crumbled up on a plate.

"Daddy?" Frances says.

Her father shakes his head.

"Can't," he says.

Frances sighs and looks at the other people. She can't imagine the cat with any of them. She can imagine it only with her.

"Maybe he belongs around here," says the young man.

"I've never seen him before," the waitress answers.

"Pretty thing," says the young man. His paperback book is lying closed beside his chili bowl.

"My wife would skin me if I brought some creature in on Christmas Eve," the big man admits to everyone who is listening.

Frances' father nods his head.

"Mine, too," he says.

Frances raises her eyebrows and looks at him, shocked. But she doesn't know why she's shocked. What he says is probably true.

She waits for the young man or the waitress to tell who is waiting

at home for them this Christmas Eve, who will skin them if they bring a creature home.

But neither speaks.

"Daddy, the waitress won't put him back outside, will she?" Frances asks her father.

"I don't know, dear."

Frances wants to know what will happen to this cat.

"At least he's fed, Frances," her father adds, taking the last drink of his coffee. "Let's hurry and get on the road."

Frances tries finishing the cherry pie, but she hasn't much appetite now. She thinks she might cry.

The big man in plaid gets up and pays for his meal, then he is gone, wishing everybody a merry Christmas as he heads out the door.

And the black cat is sleepy now. It curls itself up on a newspaper beside the cash register, its purring hard and heavy.

Humming, the waitress wipes off the countertop while the young man watches her and watches the cat.

"Looks like he's found a home," the young man says.

The waitress smiles and shakes her head.

"I don't know," she answers. "I'm not looking for a cat on Christmas Eve."

The young man shakes his head, too.

"Neither am I."

He is staring into his cold bowl of chili.

"How long are you open tonight?" he asks.

The waitress smiles again.

"Till I get tired of it, I guess."

"Let's go, Frances," says Frances' father.

While he is paying for their food, Frances is standing at the door.

She looks at the young man sitting alone at the counter, his chili cold, his book unread.

She looks at the sun-faced waitress standing at the cash register, her face moist and clear from the heat of the grill.

She looks at the black cat, its back moving up and down in long deep breathing, lying in peace on the counter.

She follows her father through the door, but as she steps outside, Frances looks back inside one more time. The young man has moved now beside the cat and he is stroking its dark fur. The waitress is talking to him and smiling as she pours him another cup of coffee. The windows are beginning to frost, hiding outside shadows. The smell of fried potatoes lingers in the air. And "Silent Night" is playing on the radio.

Frances smiles at her father, and they start for home.

For
Being Good

WHAT Philip remembers about his grandfather are the big blue veins on top of his hands. Philip hasn't seen the old man for five years, since he was six, and he can't remember his grandfather's eyes or teeth or ears or nose. Just hands with blue veins.

Grandfather is coming for Christmas, flying up from Florida. He is coming by himself because his wife, Philip's grandmother, died, and since then he's done everything alone, including celebrating Christmas. But this year he is coming to Philip's house.

Philip isn't sure he wants his grandfather to come, but he doesn't know why he feels this way. It worries him.

In the three weeks before Christmas, Philip's mother spends a lot of time shopping for Christmas presents for his grandfather. Sometimes she drags Philip along to the department store, and she squirts colognes up and down his arms, asking him to choose the best smell.

13

like a leaking bicycle tire, and he doesn't know why it is happening, and he wants to stop it. He wants to pump the old man up again, to see him wink, maybe laugh.

But Philip's grandfather sags more and more until finally he goes to bed.

Philip helps his parents clean up the kitchen.

"He misses her," his father says.

"I know," answers his mother.

"Who?" Philip asks.

And they both answer: "His wife."

Philip's father looks sad then, too, and for the first time Philip remembers that his father is talking about his own parents, his own mother, who is dead.

"Well," Philip smiles, trying to cheer him up, "he's got us."

His father hugs him then and drapes the dishtowel over his head.

When it is time for Philip to go to bed, leaving his parents to "listen for reindeer," he realizes he hasn't been thinking about presents that much at all. In fact, ever since his grandfather has arrived, he's thought mostly about him.

Halfway up the stairs Philip turns around and goes back into the kitchen. He opens the refrigerator and takes out the foil-wrapped cookie dough.

Upstairs, he stands at his grandfather's door and listens. He hears the rocking chair squeak. He hears the old man cough. So he knocks.

The door opens. His grandfather stands in his pajamas, his bald head shining, his feet bare, his blue-veined hands clutching a framed picture.

Philip holds out the foil.

"I saved you some cookie dough, Grandpa."

The old man unwraps the foil, looks at the ball of dough, then pops it into his mouth.

"Pretty good dough," he says, and he smiles.

Philip gives a little laugh. He wants to say something, to talk, but he can't think of any words.

To his surprise, his grandfather motions him into the room. He offers Philip the rocking chair, then he sits on the edge of the bed. He leans over and puts the picture into Philip's hands.

"That's your father," he says.

Philip looks at the photograph. It is a dark-haired boy, like himself. He nods his head.

"When he was a boy," the old man continues, "every Christmas Eve he'd come climbing into bed with us, Florrie and me. We never told any of his brothers, 'cause you know how boys are."

Philip grins.

"He was embarrassed about it, being so scared and nervous at Christmas that he had to crawl into our bed. We laughed about it, but we never laughed in front of him."

The old man is grinning, too. But then the grin begins to weaken.

"Truth is, we liked it." He shakes his head. "We missed having a baby in the bed between us, so we liked that little boy snoring in our ears every Christmas Eve. It was a special present just for us, we told ourselves, just for being good. Good to our boys."

Philip watches the old man's eyes fall, his mouth go slack, and even the bald head seems to lose its shine. He looks at the man's big blue veins and doesn't know what to say. So he just says "Good night" and "Merry Christmas."

In bed, Philip can't sleep. Though he thinks some about the presents he might get, mostly he thinks about the old man holding the picture of his little boy. A boy who crawled into bed and snored into his father's ear on Christmas Eve. A boy who was himself a gift to his parents, who had been good.

Philip lies awake and thinks about all this a long time. Then he leaves his bed and, going past his parents' door, he stands at his grandfather's room and knocks softly.

"Grandpa?" he whispers.

Inside, the old man mumbles.

Philip opens the door and stands beside the old man's bed.

"Grandpa," he whispers, "can I sleep with you?"

The old man mumbles again, then rolls himself to one side.

Philip climbs in.

"Good night, Grandpa," he says.

"Good night, son," is the answer.

Ballerinas
and Bears

NEW YORK is never relaxed about anything, not even Christmas Eve. When most other cities are hushed and drowsy, New York plows its way through Christmas Eve as it does all other nights—with hard jerks, with screams and groans, and with a tightness in its air.

And on Christmas Eve in New York there are wanderers. Many of them have been wanderers for years and years. But still others are new at it. They are children. And on this night, when they should be curled into a soft warm chair with a cup of cocoa, thinking about the sweet delights of Christmas morning, instead they are on the streets walking, as usual, for there is no one to be with and nothing else to do.

This Christmas Eve is a warmer one than most. There is no snow. So a young girl named Sylvia is out in the night.

She loves to walk. She has been walking at night since she was eight. What she has found out about walking is that it can bring her peace. When she waits for the walk light, she doesn't think about a small apartment full of terrible silences and shadows in its corners. When she peers in store windows, she doesn't think about the mother who is not in that apartment. When she searches the faces of other walkers, she doesn't think about the bugs and the odors she's left behind. She doesn't think about the empty refrigerator. She doesn't think about the awful emptiness of everything that should be filled to the top for a kid.

So especially on Christmas Eve she needs this walk. When nothing at home is filled to the top.

Sylvia stops at every store window that is full of toys. She knows she's too old for toys now, but she can't help looking. She mashes her face against the glass, her tongue tasting the wet mist on it, and she watches the music-box ballerinas dance, the sturdy bears drum, and the steam engines run through gingerbread tunnels.

Sylvia believes that someday in her life someone will give her one of these things for Christmas. And she will laugh and say, "Oh, but I'm too old for such foolishness now!" But she will accept the gift, the ballerina or the bear or the train, and it will mean everything to her.

Sylvia watches the faces of the people on the sidewalks. It is late, and most families are home, their children lying under soft quilts, the tree lit, the presents all wrapped. Sylvia knows this, so she knows these are not the faces of mothers and fathers she is passing. But she pretends. And she picks out the face of a particularly handsome man passing by and she imagines that he is her father and he is rushing home to her with a gold bracelet in one pocket and chocolates

of flowers and pine boughs. And the candles—hundreds of them. The church is like one big birthday cake and Sylvia imagines that she is one of the roses on top as she sits and watches the priests and the people perform.

She sits entranced, and in a while the show is ending, the priests and the people are leaving. They all move past her, then she is alone. She watches the candles for a time in the empty church, then she rises to leave.

But at the door one of the priests is standing, and he is watching her. Sylvia is frightened. She knows she shouldn't have come in. She doesn't belong in his church. He will be angry.

The priest is smiling at her, though, and he begins to walk toward her. But she runs past him, back out into the lights and the noise that make her invisible. Again she believes she is safe.

Sylvia walks.

And now she is growing tired. Now she is sleepy enough to turn toward home, to go back. She is so tired.

Sylvia steps out into the street, forgetting the walk light because she is so tired, and the yellow taxis are speeding behind her and in front of her. She is trapped. She cannot move. She stands very still and watches the cars weave all around her.

Suddenly one of the yellow taxis stops right in front of her. The window is rolled down and a young man's face, an Oriental face, looks into hers. The young man puts his hand on her arm, moving gently like a priest, and he says to her, "Don't stand in the street. It is dangerous."

His eyes, Sylvia sees, really mean it. She moves off the street carefully as he drives away.

And when she is home, Sylvia doesn't dream of ballerinas and bears.

When she is home, Sylvia falls asleep smiling into the eyes of a young man in a yellow car who put his hand on her arm and filled this Christmas Eve for her to the top.

Silver Packages

A TRAIN comes through the mountains every year at Christmas time. And though it doesn't have antlers, nor does the man standing on its rear platform have a long white beard, it may as well be Santa Claus and his sleigh for all the excitement it stirs up.

People call it the Christmas Train. And it has been coming to them for years. Each new child born in the mountains learns to walk, talk, and wait for the Christmas Train.

It is everyone's delight.

The older people remember its beginning. They tell of a rich man who had come traveling through the hills by car many years back. No one knows why he came up into the hills, but why isn't important. What matters is what happened.

The man had an accident. His car just took itself right over the side of a ridge and the man lay in that car, hurting and scared. Someone came along. Some say it was old Mr. Crookshank but others say it was Betty Pritt. But who came along isn't important either.

Whoever it was pulled that rich man out of his car and took him to a house in the hills where he was nursed and cared for until he could make it out on his own. When he left, the rich man tried to give money to the people who had helped him. But they would not accept it.

So that rich man left the mountains feeling he owed a great debt. And for the remaining years of his life, he has been repaying this debt from the caboose of a Christmas Train he brings into the hills each December.

On the twenty-third—everybody knows it—the train will slowly wind up and around the mountains, and on the platform of its caboose will stand the rich man in a blue wool coat. He will toss a sparkling silver package into the hands of each child who waits beside the tracks, and for some, it will be the only present they receive.

So the train is awfully important.

One year a boy named Frankie stands beside those tracks and waits for the Christmas Train. It is very cold and a lot of snow has come down the night before. Frankie's shoes are thin and his feet hurt badly from the cold. But he is determined to wait, even if his feet and all the rest of him become ice.

Now this particular boy wants a particular present. Not just any present tossed from the back of that train. A *particular* present: a doctor kit. He's been waiting for it, beside the tracks.

The train comes through finally. Noisy and steaming and scary, it is so big, but everyone loves to see it and they cheer and clap and some of the mothers even weep to see it coming.

Frankie stands there at the tracks, praying for a doctor kit, till he sees the caboose slowly coming up. And when it is just past his nose, he shouts and waves and runs after the train, his icy feet aching.

From the rear platform, the rich man in the wool coat sees him. "Merry Christmas!" he calls.

And he tosses into Frankie's hands a sparkling silver package.

Frankie stops running. He is out of breath so he can't yell a thank-you. He can only hold tight to his gift and wave to the man and the train disappearing into the mountains.

Frankie carries his package home, and puts his own name on it, and sets it under the family Christmas tree. On Christmas morning, he opens it.

It isn't a doctor kit. It's a cowboy holster set and three pairs of thick red socks.

Frankie looks at his mother and father and brothers and sisters and tries not to cry.

He wears the socks all winter and plays with the cowboy set all year. But he dreams of a doctor kit.

The next Christmas Frankie waits again in the cold for the Christmas Train. The socks still fit him, so his feet are warm. But his fingers are cold and hurting.

He waits at the tracks and prays for a doctor kit. The train comes, the rich man tosses the silver package.

And on Christmas morning, Frankie opens it.

No.

It is a little police car with lights that really work plus two pairs of brown mittens.

Frankie doesn't cry.

He wears the mittens all winter and plays with the car all year. But he dreams of a doctor kit.

Frankie waits three more years for a doctor kit. It never comes.

He gets trucks and balls and games. He gets mittens and socks and hats and scarves.

But the doctor kit never comes.

When Frankie grows up, he moves away, out of the hills. He lives in different places and meets different kinds of people and he himself changes a little into a different kind of person.

But deep in him, never changing, are his memories. And what he remembers most about being a boy in the hills is that just when it seemed his feet would freeze like the snow, a man on a train had brought socks. Just when it seemed his fingers were hardening to ice, the man had brought mittens. Just when the cold wind was cutting sharp as a blade into his throat, the man had brought a scarf. And just when Frankie's ears were numb with red cold, the man had brought a hat.

And Frankie remembers something about owing a debt.

So, a grown man who has been gone a long time moves back into those same mountains to live. His brothers and sisters are still there, waiting for him.

He returns to the hills where he has grown up, and that winter, near Christmas, he stands at the tracks, watching the children wait for the train.

And it comes, as always.

The grown man watches the steam engine move toward him, watches the caboose roll by him, and he nearly runs after that train, so strong are his memories. This grown man nearly runs after a silver package.

But instead he watches a little girl chase that caboose, watches a man in a wool coat toss her a sparkling silver package, watches the gift land near the little girl's feet, watches her running so fast that she trips on her silver package, watches her fall hard to the ground.

The grown man does run now, but not for a train. Not for a rich man in a wool coat. For a little girl.

He picks her up from the gravel. He wipes away her tears with the scarf from around his neck. He smiles at her.

"It's okay, little one," he says easily. The train is disappearing into the trees. He had meant to wave to the rich man. But there wasn't time.

He picks up the silver package and puts it into the little girl's arms.

"You'll be all right," he tells her. "I'll make sure."

He pulls open his kit to look for a Band-Aid.

"Name's Frank," he smiles. "I'm a doctor."

All the Stars in the Sky

EVERYBODY knows Mae. She's been on the streets for years. She has wild eyes and nobody trusts her. She wears stinking clothes and nobody approaches her. She enjoys garbage cans and nobody likes her.

Nobody but her dogs.

She has three of them but only one has a name. She calls it Marty. The other two she speaks to, and feeds when she has food. But no names.

Mae has been in town for so many years that no one notices her anymore. She's like the old department store downtown that's boarded up and full of empty shelves and dusty dress racks. Nobody looks at that old department store on his way home or to school or to work or out to the mall where the new department store is. Nobody looks at the old store anymore and nobody looks at Mae.

Mae has been doing fair, though, these many years she's been on the streets. She knows where to go when she is hungry enough to ask for food. The church downtown has given free lunches every day at noon for as long as she can remember. She knows she won't starve to death. And if she has to, she knows where she can sleep in a bed, inside a building. The Mission Home always lets people like Mae in at night to rest, if they want in. But they can stay only the night. In the morning they have to leave, have to go out on their own again.

Some of them can remember when they had homes. They can remember when they were living with a family and sleeping in their pajamas in their own beds in a house that was warm and had food in its cabinets.

The ones who can remember this suffer most. Because they know what it is not to sleep on a park bench or a sidewalk. They know the smell of clean blankets. They know the taste of fresh milk and fried eggs every morning.

They know something about being loved.

But Mae knows none of this. Mae knows which garbage cans have the best scraps after the dinner hour. She knows which shops throw out old clothes and when they are thrown out. She knows where to find a good clean newspaper if the wind is cold and she needs cover at night. She knows how to find the church and the Mission Home. She knows her dog Marty's name.

But everything else she has forgotten.

This year, this winter, this December, Mae needs to remember something. She needs very badly to remember it, but she can't. She walks her daily route, the three dogs following and sniffing at every piece of garbage, every color on the street, but Mae doesn't search

RETA E. KING LIBRARY
CHADRON STATE COLLEGE
CHADRON, NE 69337

the cans this day in December. She walks very slowly with her hands deep down in the pockets of her dirty coat, her hair flying and her wild eyes full of tears.

She is sick. And she can't remember where to go.

Mae knows there is a place. She's been sick once before, when a boy on a bike knocked her down and suddenly people noticed her, the dirty old woman lying at their feet. Someone had come for her and she'd been taken to a place for sick people and made well and fed six times.

Where is it now?

Mae needs the sick place.

She walks with her dogs and cries.

She walks all day with her head held down and she doesn't see the lights of the stores flashing green and red and the pine trees in the store windows shining with gold balls and silver beads and the people walking fast all around her with their big bags and boxes, pulling small children behind them, saying, "Hurry, the stores are about to close."

She doesn't see Santa on the corner.

Mae just walks, her head hung low, her dogs there.

Finally it is nearly dark and she is so sick and so very tired that she gives up walking, looking for the sick place. She shuffles into an alleyway and drops in front of a large metal door, the side entrance of a building. Marty and the other two dogs sit down, waiting to see what Mae will do next.

Mae wipes her wet face with her sleeve and pulls her coat tighter around her. Then she gives a great sigh and leans back against the door. And as she leans, the door creaks loud and it opens up so quickly that Mae falls backwards right into the building.

Mae yells and Marty and the two dogs bark and there is nothing but confusion for a time. But then, Mae gets up off the floor and realizes no one has come. There are empty desks and boxes of books on the floor. No one has come.

So Mae closes herself and the three dogs inside that building. She shuts the metal door and it bangs hard and then there is nothing but desks and books and dogs and Mae.

Mae wonders if she has found the sick place after all. She shivers and walks toward the door at the end of the room. She thinks that when she opens it she will see the sick place and everything will be better.

But when she opens it and looks out, there is no sick place. Only a room that a giant might live in, and it is full of books. Rows and rows of shelves. Thousands and thousands of books.

A book place.

Mae leans against the wall and looks at all those books and knows where she is. She's come in this building before, to get warm. She can sit at a table and be warm and no one will tell her to leave.

They are all gone today, the book people. No one but Mae.

She moves. The dogs follow.

Mae finds some other rooms with desks. She finds a bathroom. A closet.

And then she finds a kitchen. Mae goes in like a child, into that kitchen, so hungry. She finds food. Mae finds sandwiches and cookies and a big jar of peanut butter and some milk and apples and cheese and even a box of candy. Mae puts it all on the floor. She puts every bit of food she finds on the floor, then she and Marty and the two dogs do nothing but eat for a very long time.

Then Mae, full and feeling sleepy, curls into a ball on the floor, and Marty and the two dogs curl into balls against Mae, and they all sleep.

When Mae wakes up it is so dark she can't see even her hands and she is afraid and calls out. The dogs bark and bark and Mae stumbles into the darkness, slipping on the food on the floor, then remembering where she is. She finds a light switch.

Mae wanders from room to room again. The giant room with books is lit by a few dim lights, so she doesn't have to look for any more switches. The dogs trot up and down the rows of books and their toenails make clicks on the tile floor, small clicks that sound loud and important in the empty spaces.

Mae finds a stairway and she can see well enough so she goes up. She is feeling better.

At the top is another room full of books and shelves but this room is different. It has an aquarium in it that buzzes low in the half-dark and makes the walls of the room look liquid. Mae walks over to it and presses her hands against the glass and watches the fish swim. She stands there a long time.

Then she moves around the room. There are pictures all over the walls, full of color, and things hang down from the ceiling, paper things on strings. Mae wants one but she can't reach it. There is a Christmas tree in the room. Mae knows what that is but she is afraid of them. Marty and the dogs sniff at it, though.

Mae finds some large, soft cushions on the floor and she curls herself into one and watches the fish and the liquid lights on the walls.

The dogs lie down beside her. Mae whistles low to Marty and he wags his tail.

On the floor next to her cushion, Mae sees a basket of books.

They are very shiny and at first she is afraid. But finally she picks one up.

It is a book about a snowman, Mae can see that. It is easy for her since it has no words, only pictures. Mae turns the pages and watches the snowman come to life and fly in the sky with a boy beside him. She watches the snowman melt on the last page and nods her head yes then picks up another book.

It has words, so Mae nearly puts it back down, but the pictures of the woman and the baby and all the stars in the sky hold her and Mae turns the pages slowly, curled into her cushion, and breathes deep and quiet, and looks.

Mae looks at every book in the basket while her dogs sleep. Every Christmas book in the basket.

Then she lays her head against Marty and she sleeps, too.

In the morning, Mae and her dogs leave the book place. She can't stay. She doesn't want to be found.

She leaves behind the books and the fish and even the food on the kitchen floor. And when she opens the door that had so suddenly let her inside the night before, Mae is surprised at how quiet the streets are. She and Marty and the two dogs come out of the alley and there are hardly any cars and no buses and few people. The stores are all closed.

Mae walks with her dogs, her stomach full, not sick anymore, and a sign in a store window says "Merry Christmas!" but Mae sees only a snowman flying and a woman and a baby and stars and stars and stars.